TONY JOHNSTON

Fishing Sunday

pictures by BARRY ROOT

TAMBOURINE BOOKS NEW YORK

For James Tanaka
T.J.

For Golda Laurens
B.R.

Printed in Hong Kong by South China Printing Company (1988) Ltd.
The text type is Schneidler. The illustrations were painted in
watercolor and gouache on paper.

Library of Congress Cataloging in Publication Data
Johnston, Tony, 1942–   Fishing Sunday / by Tony Johnston ;
illustrated by Barry Root. — 1st ed.   p. cm. Summary: A young boy
is embarrassed by his grandfather's old Japanese ways, but on one of
their Fishing Sundays, he learns to see Grandfather in a new light.
[1. Grandfathers—Fiction. 2. Japanese Americans—Fiction.
3. Fishing—Fiction.] I. Root, Barry, ill. II. Title.
PZ7.J6478Fj 1996 [E]—dc20 95-30632   CIP   AC
ISBN 0-688-13458-0

1 3 5 7 9 10 8 6 4 2
First edition

Fishing Sunday, Grandfather calls it. It's the day that I hate most.

Our house is as dark as a cricket. And still. Then I hear the shuffle of my grandfather's tough old feet.

In the quiet he squawks, "Fishing Sunday! Fishing Sunday!" all excited like a silly sea gull.

I groan, but rise and dress.

We eat breakfast, then gather our things. Grandfather gets the bamboo pole that he made himself. Fishhooks, too, made from bones he found in the garbage. He carries them gently, like eggs, as we hurry along.

Grandfather is old and stooped, his skin brown from too much sun. His clothes are shabby, always the same. Blue shirt and pants, too short, like he suddenly grew in a spurt. The worst thing is his feet. His toenails are sharp and split and black. But he will not wear shoes.

"Feet like air," he says.

Grandfather and I are like two odd birds—him blue and bare-foot, me colorful with tennis shoes—trudging over the sand.

I think he would like to hold my hand. But I rush ahead to see what he calls "small gifts of the tide." Rags of kelp, stiff with salt. Broken clamshells, black and shiny inside. Crabs stumbling along.

I always go slow, hoping to miss the fishing boat, but we never do.

When Grandfather sees the people, he calls, "Fishing Sunday!"
Then he grins, and his missing teeth show.

The people shout back. They smile too. I know what their
smiles mean. *Here comes that old Japanese fool. The only English
he knows is "Fishing Sunday." And he fishes with bones. Look at his
ugly feet. Why doesn't he wear shoes?*

When someone stares at his feet, Grandfather says, "Feet like
air."

I have a favorite fishing place, a sea-snake coil of rope in a
corner where it's dark. Nobody sees me there.

But does Grandfather fish in a corner? No. His favorite spot is
plop in the middle of everyone, by a big man with a bushy red
beard and eyebrows the same.

"Fishing Sunday!" cries Grandfather, arranging his line.

"FISHING SUNDAY!" booms the man.

Before, I said the worst thing about Grandfather is his feet. That's not true. The worst thing is—he talks to the fish, babbles to the whole oceanful!

"Come fish. Come to me. Please let me catch you." Then, after the small commotion of a catch, he stares into the fish's eyes and says, "Thank you, fish, for this deep honor."

Everyone can hear. I feel deep red burn my ears.

Today is Fishing Sunday again. Grandfather and I rush along, egg-walking our gear. As usual, he offers his hand, but I run to see the hull of a boat, washed up like great fish bones. Grandfather scuttles to the top. His brown legs dangle down. His black toenails shine. Soon the people will smile at him, and stare. I wish I could stay here.

Now we are fishing, out on the sea, bobbing like a big white gull. I am in my coiled corner, but Grandfather is in full view, grinning at everyone, casting—*whip, whip*—with his bamboo pole, chattering, "Come fish. Come to me. Please let me catch you."

He is catching fish, too—more than anyone. They squirm at his feet in flashes of silver.

Then I hear another voice. Not Grandfather's, thin as a fish bone, but a deep boom.

"COME FISH! COME TO ME! PLEASE LET ME CATCH YOU!"

Soon Red Beard catches a fish. He thanks it, too, but booming.

I long to catch a fish, to feel it tug my line, to reel it in and cook it for supper.

No one is watching, so I whisper, "Come fish. Come to me. Please let me catch you."

No fish come, so I whisper louder. Still, nothing happens.

Someone hears me. Beside me is Grandfather, his eyes, bright as a fish's, smiling.

"No fish." I shrug, lifting my empty line.

"Fish talk takes time," he says. "With words of respect, they will come."

He takes something from his pocket and slides it into my hand. A fishhook made from bone, polished by his hands. I see that it is beautiful.

When he goes, I tie the fishhook to a piece of line and slip it around my neck, so a fish won't swallow it.

I pretend to fish, but really I watch Grandfather. I watch him smile and talk to the fish.

Grandfather is old and stooped, his skin brown like kelp. His clothes are tattered blue, like sky above the sea. When he speaks, his words are crabs stumbling along. His toenails are broken clamshells, split and sharp and black. My grandfather is the sea itself.

For the first time I see that he is beautiful.

On the way home we are walking like two odd birds. I stop and kick off my shoes. I look at Grandfather and say, "Feet like air."

We laugh. And I take his hand.